Biscuit

Phonics Fun

I Can Read Book® is a trademark of HarperCollins Publishers.
This Is Biscuit
Biscuit and the Cat
Biscuit and the Hen
Biscuit's Tub Fun
Biscuit's Trick
Biscuit and the Box
Biscuit and Sam
Biscuit and the Nest
Biscuit and the Duck
Biscuit and the Kittens
Biscuit and the Frog
Biscuit

ISBN 978-0-06-243638-2

First Edition

15 16 17 18 19 SCP 10 9 8 7 6 5 4 3 2 1

I Can Read! **Phonics**

Biscuit
Phonics Fun

stories by Alyssa Satin Capucilli

pictures by Pat Schories

Table of Contents

Letter to Parents and Teachers

Dear Parents and Teachers,

Welcome to the I Can Read! phonics program. Your child is about to start an exciting adventure. He or she is going to learn to read. By choosing one of your child's favorite characters, you have already accomplished something very important—motivation!

Biscuit Phonics Fun includes twelve stories, planned by a phonics expert. The stories are intended for children to read at home with a parent or caregiver and, eventually, by themselves.

- *Biscuit Phonics Fun* introduces the short vowel sounds **a**, **e**, **i**, **o**, and **u**. One of the key components in becoming a fluent reader is practice, so this set features two stories for each sound, plus one introductory story, and one story that reinforces all the sounds. Learning to read short vowels is rewarding because they are found everywhere!
- Fun Biscuit words have been included to make the stories rich and enjoyable.
- The stories also include sight words. These are words frequently found in books that can be hard to sound out. They just need to be learned by sight!
- Picture clues support the text in each story and help children learn new words.

As children master the sounds and words, they will gain experience and confidence in their ability to understand sounds, sound out words, and READ! Here are some suggestions for using *Biscuit Phonics Fun* to help your child on the road to reading:

1. Read the books aloud to your child. The first time you read a story, read it all the way through. Then invite your child to follow along by pointing out words as you read them. Encourage him or her to try to sound out new words that use familiar sounds, or that are pictured in the illustrations.

2. Discuss each sound found on the first page with your child. Help your child sound out the new words in the story. Demonstrate the vowel sounds—for example, by telling your child that the short **o** vowel sound is found in the word **hot**.

3. Look at the pictures with your child. Encourage him or her to tell the story through the pictures. Point out objects in the pictures and ask your child to name them.

We hope that you and your child enjoy *Biscuit Phonics Fun*, and that it is the start of many happy reading adventures.

The HarperCollins Editors

This Is Biscuit

Book 1
Introduction

In this story you will learn new sight words. Can you find these words?

this   is   and   has

lots   of   the   a   all

Here are some fun Biscuit words:

Biscuit   small   yellow

friends   duck   Sam

big   woof   little

girl   best

This is Biscuit.

Biscuit is small
and yellow.

Biscuit has lots of friends.

The duck is a small friend.

Sam is a big friend.

Woof!
The little girl is Biscuit's
best friend of all!

Biscuit and the Cat

Book 2
Short a

In this story you will learn about the **short a** vowel sound. Can you find these words and sound them out?

ran   cat   mat   naps   can

Here are some new sight words:

to   the   on

Here are some fun Biscuit words:

Biscuit   woof

Biscuit ran.

Biscuit ran to the cat.

The cat ran to the mat.

The cat naps on the mat.

Woof! Can Biscuit nap?

Nap, nap, cat.

Nap, nap, Biscuit.

Biscuit and the Hen

Book 3
Short e

In this story you will learn about the **short e** vowel sound. Can you find these words and sound them out?

met   **pen**   **went**
hen   **get**   **peck**

Here are some review sight words:

a   **the**   **of**

Here are some new sight words:

was   **out**   **in**   **said**

Here are some fun words:

Biscuit   **woof**

Biscuit met a hen.

The hen was out
of the pen.

Get in the pen, hen.

Biscuit went in the pen.

The hen went in the pen.

Woof! said Biscuit.
Peck, Peck!
went the hen.

Biscuit's Tub Fun

Book 4
Short u

In this story you will learn about the **short u** vowel sound. Can you find these words and sound them out?

dug	**fun**	**tug**
mud	**rub-a-dub**	**tub**

Here are some review sight words:

in   the   a   to

Here are some new sight words:

is   for   it

Here are some fun words:

Biscuit   time   woof   more

Biscuit dug.

Biscuit dug in the mud.

The mud is fun!

Rub-a-dub.

Time for a tub!

It is fun to tug.

Woof!

It is time for more tub fun.

Biscuit's Trick

Book 5
Short i

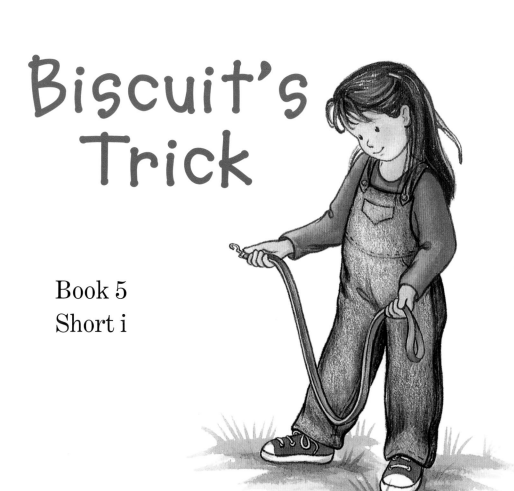

In this story you will learn about the **short i** vowel sound. Can you find these words and sound them out?

sit   **pick**   **stick**   **give**   **trick**
dig   **big**   **did**   **kiss**

Here are some review sight words:

a   **it**

Here are some new sight words:

can   **up**

Here are some fun words:

Biscuit   **woof**   **good**

Biscuit can sit.

Biscuit can dig.

Can Biscuit pick up
a big stick?

Biscuit did it.
A big stick!

Biscuit can give a kiss.

Woof!
Biscuit did
a good trick.

Biscuit and the Box

Book 6
Short o

In this story you will learn about the **short o** vowel sound. Can you find these words and sound them out?

box   got   dog
hop   plop   not

Here are some review sight words:

a   was   in   the   can

Here are some new sight words:

saw

Here are some fun words:

Biscuit   bunny   woof

Biscuit saw a box.

A bunny was in the box.

Hop, hop, hop.

Biscuit got in the box.

Hop, hop, hop.
PLOP!

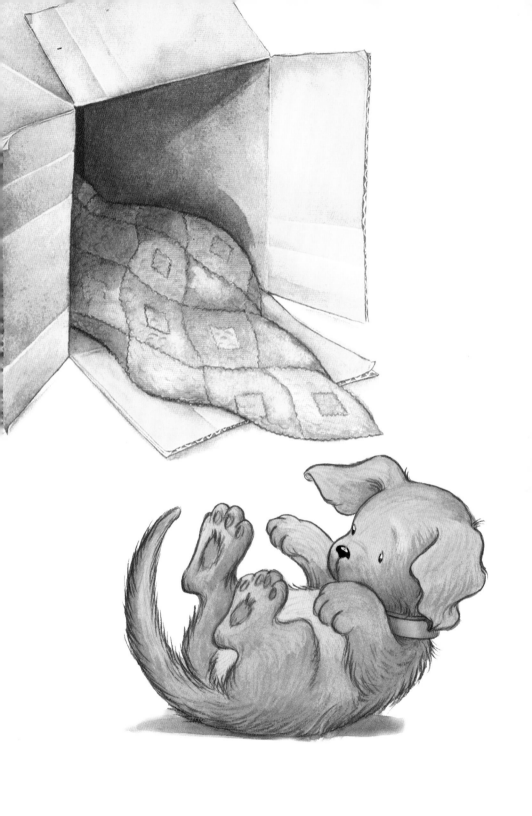

Woof!
A dog can
not hop!

Biscuit and Sam

Book 7
Short a

In this story you will learn about the **short a** vowel sound. Can you find these words and sound them out?

Sam   **fast**   **carry**   **pal**
can   **catch**   **branch**

Here are some review sight words:

a   **is**

Here are some new sight words:

too

Here are some fun words:

run   **ball**   **woof**   **Biscuit**   **ruff**   **help**

Sam can run fast.

Sam can catch a ball.

Sam can carry a branch.

Woof!

Can Biscuit carry
a branch, too?

Ruff!

Sam can help Biscuit.

Sam is Biscuit's pal!

Biscuit and the Nest

Book 8
Short e

In this story you will learn about the **short e** vowel sound. Can you find these words and sound them out?

egg   **nest**   **help**   **set**   **pet**
fell   **get**   **went**   **best**

Here are some review sight words:

the   **for**   **in**

Here are some new sight words:

an   **from**   **saw**   **you**   **are**

Here are some fun words:

Biscuit   **woof**   **little**   **girl**   **she**

An egg fell

from the nest.

Get help, Biscuit!

Woof!

Biscuit went for help.

The little girl saw the egg.

She set the egg
in the nest.

"You are the best pet, Biscuit!"

Biscuit and the Duck

Book 9
Short u

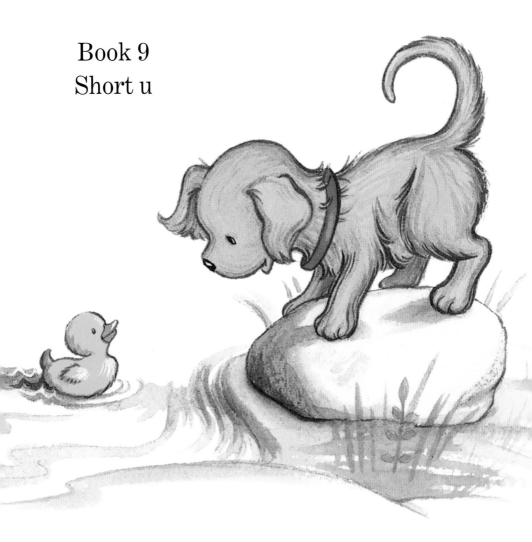

In this story you will learn about the **short u** vowel sound. Can you find these words and sound them out?

sun   **duck**   **fun**   **run**
up   **jumped**   **pups**

Here are some review sight words:

the   **was**   **in**   **are**   **too**

Here are some new sight words:

like

Here are some fun words:

puddle   **quack**   **woof**

The sun was up.

The duck jumped
in the puddle.

Quack!
Puddles are fun.

Woof!

Pups like puddles, too.

Run, run, run, jump!

Duck fun. Pup fun.
Puddle fun!

Biscuit and the Kittens

Book 10
Short i

In this story you will learn about the **short i** vowel sound. Can you find these words and sound them out?

will   filled   milk   sip
dish   with   kittens

Here are some review sight words:

be   in   the   is   for   like

Here are some fun words:

what   woof   Biscuit   mew

What will be in the dish?

Woof!

The dish is filled
with milk.

Is the milk for Biscuit?

Mew!

The milk is for the kittens.

Sip, sip.

Kittens like milk.

Mew!

The kittens like Biscuit.

Biscuit and the Frog

Book 11
Short o

In this story you will learn about the **short o** vowel sound. Can you find these words and sound them out?

frog   on   hot   stop   dog
hopped   log   top   drop

Here are some review sight words:

saw   a   the   it   was   of

Here are some new sight words:

off

Here are some fun words:

Biscuit   woof   drip   silly

Biscuit saw a frog.

The frog hopped
on the log.

It was hot on top
of the log.

The frog hopped off.

Stop, Biscuit, stop!

Woof!
Drip, drop!
Silly dog!

Biscuit

Book 12
Review

In this story you will review the short vowel sounds. Can you find these words and sound them out?

this   his   rag   box   all   fun
is   bed   doll   best   have   with

Here are some sight words:

likes   of   to

Here are some fun words:

Biscuit   ball   biscuits   friends

This is Biscuit.

Biscuit likes his bed.

Biscuit likes his ball.

Biscuit likes his rag doll.

Biscuit likes his
box of biscuits.

Best of all, Biscuit likes
to have fun with his friends!